PARADISE FOUND

John Milton
Illustrations Helen Elliott

Paradise Found.
Published in Great Britain in 2018
by Graffeg Limited

Written by John Milton copyright © 2018.
Illustrated by Helen Elliott copyright © 2018.
Designed and produced by Graffeg Limited
copyright © 2018

Graffeg Limited, 24 Stradey Park Business Centre,
Mwrwg Road, Llangennech, Llanelli,
Carmarthenshire SA14 8YP Wales UK
Tel 01554 824000 www.graffeg.com

ISBN 9781912213641

1 2 3 4 5 6 7 8 9

PARADISE FOUND

John Milton
Illustrations Helen Elliott

This book belongs to

_____

_____

_____

GRAFFEG

'Hey up there Albie' said Ma as she woke Albie with a gentle kick, 'fire's nearly out!'

Ma knelt down putting one hand on Albie and the other hand onto a log. She clanked open the fire door, roused the fire with the iron poker and tossed a hefty log into the flames. She pushed down heavily on Albie to get to her feet. 'Sleepy dog,' said Ma in a warm voice, 'don't sleep all day.'

Albie loved the kitchen. It was always filled with the smell of food. A smell that seemed to soak into everything, but he especially loved the fire. He was always to be found laid on his back, paws in the air basking in its orange glow. The fire was always alive and rarely allowed to go out, because of this the stone floor in the kitchen was always warm.

Logs were neatly stacked at either side of the fire, Albie liked the smell of the wood, it smelled of outside and he sniffed every new piece brought into the house from the wood store. Sometimes he would try and catch the stowaway spiders that would scurry across the kitchen floor from the logs to escape the fire.

Albie stretched and let out a long yawn, stood up back legs first with tail in the air and front legs straight forward, scratching the stone floor with his nails as he drew them in and came to his feet. He shook his head and wagged his tail, trotted over to his and Nellie's bowls; he sniffed both, Albie's bowl was licked clean, but Nellie's food was untouched! Albie sniffed the biscuits again, lifted his head and looked around the kitchen. Where was Nellie?

The kitchen door was open and Albie could hear the blackbirds in the garden, he took a quick look back at the fire and walked out into the morning sun. The blackbirds chirruped and made for the safety of the hawthorn trees at the bottom of the garden. Albie would never bother the blackbirds but they always scattered with a fuss whenever he came into the garden.

He walked along the garden path, past the vegetable patch with its neat rows of carrots and parsnips, all the way past the greenhouse, full of strung up tomato plants weighed down with ripening yellow and orange tomatoes, right down to the hawthorn trees where the blackbirds now perched, looking down at him. He sniffed around the huge dark green rhubarb leaves that grew up against the garden wall, but couldn't see Nellie anywhere!

Albie scrambled up the old stone wall behind the hawthorn trees that bordered the garden and the meadow at the back of the house. The meadow was a deep emerald green spattered all over with buttercups, daisies, dandelions and hemlock.

Sometimes large brown cows grazed the meadow and would occasionally put their heads over the garden wall to eat Ma's sweet peas off the trellis. Ma would come rushing down the garden like a bumblebee, shooing them away with a tea towel. But there were no cows today, just the breeze making waves in the grass as it blew gently across the meadow.

Away down the rolling slope of the meadow, down towards the sea Albie could hear the rattle of farmer Jones' tractor as he cut the meadow for hay. He startled the blackbirds once more as he leapt from the stonewall into the ocean of swaying grass and headed down the hill to the sea. Maybe Nellie was playing on the beach? Albie thought to himself.

Albie ran down the hill and through the long meadow grass, flushing out butterflies and grasshoppers as he went, springing up above the grass every now and then to check his surroundings, just like the dolphins that leapt clear of the water when they accompanied the fishing boats out of the harbour. Albie raced through the long grass and shot out behind farmer Jones' tractor and right into the freshly mowed path he'd cut. The smell of the freshly cut meadow grass filled the air and Albie paused, lifted his head and sniffed the breeze.

Farmer Jones was sitting almost side-saddle on the tractor and constantly checking his path, half the time looking forward and half the time back at the cut. Albie caught his eye and the old man raised his fingers to his lips, letting out a high pitched whistle. Albie pricked up his ears and looked towards the smiling farmer sitting across his tractor, then turned and ran down along the heaps of cut grass and out of the meadow to the cliffs.

A narrow path ran all the way along the cliff tops, up and down the rolling hills until it reached a short drop down to the beach. Albie splashed through the cold shallow stream that ran out across one side of the beach. The tide was almost right out and the beach was deserted, he ran out onto the wide-open space of the beach and sniffed at the fresh sea air.

Albie found some fresh paw prints in the sand, but they weren't Nellie's, they were too big and wide. Nellie's were narrower, just like Albie's. Nellie was slightly shorter than Albie but otherwise they were very alike. Dusty white all over with black patches over both eyes, the only difference being that Albie wore a blue collar where Nellie's was red. Albie loved Nellie! Where was she?

He ran back along the shoreline, scaring the seagulls to flight that were wading through the shallow waves that gently stroked the flat sand. The seagulls' cries carried across the bay as they hung in the breeze, they would all return to the tide line once Albie was gone. Albie's long legs were wet and sandy but his head and tail were fairly dry.

He shook himself and ran across the empty beach towards the cobblestone slipway. Fishermen used to bring small boats down the slipway to the beach and the big old stones were brown and black with scars from years of use. Albie made short work of the stones as he ran up the slipway and onto the quay. He looked across the wide beach from the height of the quay, but Nellie wasn't anywhere to be seen, just the sand, the sea, and the sky.

Albie trotted past the harbour, where the boats were now high and dry. Some of the boats had stayed upright on their keels in the mud, whilst many of the others were just laid over, waiting for the tide to turn and pick them up once more. The small flags and wires on their masts ticked and clinked in the wind.

Away up the high street, an impatient car horn made Albie's head turn. 'Hmm', he thought, and headed for the town.

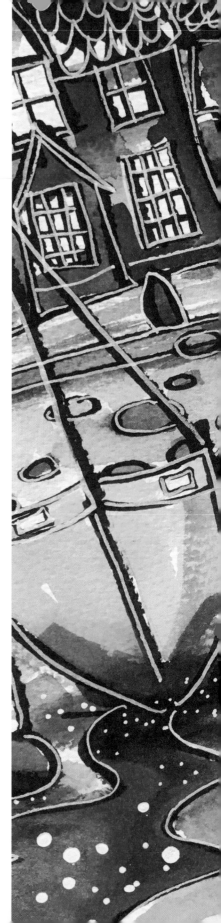

The high street was bustling with townsfolk and its pavements were full. It was lined with brightly painted shops and houses of blues, pale pinks and turquoise.

Shops had their wares stacked out onto the street underneath red and blue heavy canvas canopies, greengrocers with their fruit and vegetables in boxes on trestles with fake grass. Cafes with iron tables and chairs that rattled on the path. Albie passed unnoticed through the maze of tables, pushchairs and shoppers. 'Surely Nellie wouldn't come this way?' he thought.

It was at that very moment that his sandy nose met with a very interesting smell drifting along the path. Led on by the intoxicating aroma, Albie followed his nose all the way down the street and to the corner, where Owain the butcher was proudly displaying a window full of the best local produce.

Owain, a pompous fat man full of his own importance, was busy. He had a shop full and the queue was running to the doorway. 'Next!' shouted Owain, rubbing his hands together and another customer approached the counter. The whiff was absolutely irresistible.

Albie saw his chance and launched himself right into the window display. Sliding and running on the spot as his feet slipped on the polished stainless steel shelf, as he spun around he sent chops, sausages and pies flying in all directions. The long queue let out a synchronised gasp and backed away from the unfolding disaster in the window.

At first, only Owain's eyes darted sharply left, until a second later the big man swung around. 'Whaaat the arrrrrrgh!' bellowed a very red faced Owain as he dived headlong into his own window display causing far more devastation than Albie ever had. As the exploding butcher scrambled for traction in the window amongst the trays of tripe and liver, Albie's canines connected with a string of plump pork 'Owain's own special recipe' sausages.

Albie was airborne and out of the door like a rocket, but Owain wasn't far behind. The furious butcher chased Albie all the way up the street, shouting with every giant step and clearing flagstones three at a time. Now purple faced with rage and knocking over the cafe chairs as he went.

He made a last desperate lunge for the dog, coming down heavily in the road. His chunky right hand catching the end of the flailing sausages, snapping them in two and leaving Albie to make good his escape with a single sausage clamped in his jaws.

Albie left the still fuming butcher laid in the road tightly holding the sausages and ran as fast as he could for the fields and hills behind the town. He didn't stop until he was far, far away from trouble. Albie sat there panting until eventually he got his breath back. 'Hmmph' he sniffed, 'I don't think Nellie will be in the high street'.

Some way up the hill behind the town was the old railway line. The old steam trains used to run coal from the mine down to the docks in long lines of wagons made of iron and wood. The mine had long since closed, but the railway had found a new lease of life running tourists on sightseeing trips through the hills and mountains.

Albie used to come up here with Nellie when they were out together. Maybe she was here? Had she come out to chase the hordes of rabbits that lived up here? The numerous rabbits burrowed into the ash that the old wooden railway sleepers rested on and there were holes everywhere. Albie slowly walked up to the line sniffing at a large rabbit warren entrance, but he wasn't interested in rabbits today. He had to find Nellie.

Just a short distance along the track, a rather pretty looking small green steam locomotive was being readied for the day and it was shooting steam from the drain cocks near its wheels. Steam was blasting out of both sides of the engine before disappearing. Albie could hear the fireman and the engineer talking about the day ahead. The engineer blew the engine's whistle and white steam shot up into the air. A long 'tooooot!' echoed off the hillside.

Albie trotted over to see what was going on. He jumped up the cast iron steps and walking up to the fireman, he sat down at his feet. The fireman was sitting on the footplate with the fire door open, drinking tea from a large and dirty white mug. Albie could see the coal blazing in the firebox, it reminded him of the fire at home in the kitchen. With the red of the fire shining in his eyes he thought about Nellie. The footplate was black and brightly polished from years of coal being shovelled from the tender into the firebox. The white-haired fireman was surprised to see Albie there.

'Hello boy what are you looking for?' he said, placing a hand black with coal on Albie's back and leaving a black hand print as he did so. 'Nothing to eat up here boy' he declared with a smile.

Albie licked the fireman's black face, revealing a swarthy pink cheek under the coal dust. The fireman shook as he laughed, spilling tea onto his boots.

Albie jumped down onto the track, barking at the hissing steam as he hurried off over the lines and into the bracken.

The old railway line marked the boundary of the end of farmland from where Albie had come and the rocky, wild countryside that led up the hillside to the mountains. At the other side of the railway the hill became much steeper and rugged, with only islands of coarse grass and heather covering the otherwise bare black rock.

Albie headed along the stony hill path thinking about Nellie. He'd never been apart from Nellie for this long, they were always together, by the fire in the kitchen or barking at the blackbirds in the garden. Sometimes they even played hide and seek in the long meadow grass at the back of the house, but always together.

Trotting along and thinking to himself he noticed a very small wisp of white smoke coming from a narrow opening in the hillside up ahead. Albie came to the small hole in the rock and breathed in the pale smoke. It wasn't sooty or nasty like the smoke from the steam loco fire, but sweet and fresh. The hole was quite small but big enough for Albie to squeeze through.

Once inside it revealed a roughly round tunnel, hewn from the black rock and with a narrow flat stony floor. Albie followed the path for some time, it twisted and turned as it went.

Albie was suddenly afraid and thought of turning back to the daylight and the warm summer day he'd left behind. But the ribbon of thin white smoke that floated along the path seemed to draw him onwards and downwards. It was taking him deep down into the heart of the mountain. After what seemed like a long time, the path opened out into a very large and dimly lit chamber.

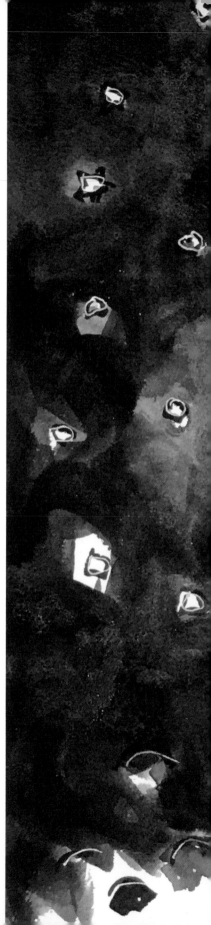

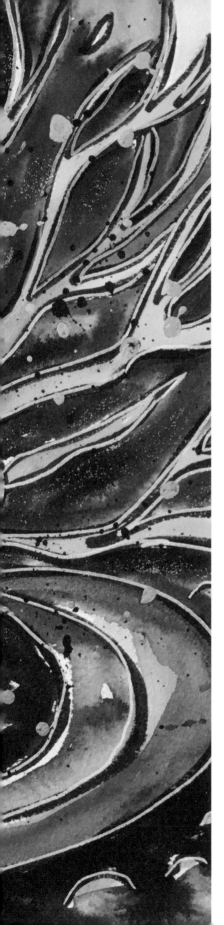

The chamber was quite spacious and lit only by the veins of glistening quartz and gold that marbled the walls. Albie was standing in the half-light waiting for his eyes to get accustomed to the dark when he heard faint whispering and thought he saw something moving his way in the darkness. He heard a heavy wheezy breathing when out of the gloom came a pair of yellow, reptile-like eyes. These belonged to a very, very old dragon called Gwendolyn, as old as the mountain itself. She was ancient and small, smaller than Albie, with deep blood-red smooth scales that pointed backwards and ran over her entire body. Her tail arched up in the air and over her body, the tip of which hung constantly just above her head pointing forwards, her dark yellow eyes only made her scaly skin look deeper red.

Gwendolyn was a kind dragon though and she didn't guard heaps of diamonds and gold coins like most dragons, but the sparkling gold in the walls was hers and she guarded it just the same from men that might want to dig it out.

Gwendolyn shuffled around the chamber in a figure of eight, never taking her eyes away from Albie, muttering and whispering to herself, until after a short while Gwendolyn came right up to Albie's face and looked deep into his brown eyes holding him transfixed in her gaze. 'Sssss ...I ... see ... everything!', she hissed slowly, letting out a small wisp of white smoke as she spoke. She paused for a minute and spoke again, 'your eyes tell me that you are looking for someone, someone special, I can help you if you'd like?'

Her yellow eyes opened wide and then narrowed as she looked directly at him. A smile slowly spread all the way along her snout revealing her razor-sharp teeth. Breathing out her white dragon smoke, she spoke:

'She's right up in the top, laid asleep in the gold,
with the owl and the mice looking on so I'm told.'
'She's waiting for you and there's five maybe more,
in farmer Jones' barn, put your nose round the door.'
'So run like the wind so you'll not be too late,
quick as you can dog, go find your mate!'

Nellie! Farmer Jones! That's why he whistled!

Albie could no longer see the old dragon in the smoky chamber. He barked in thanks, turned and ran back up the dark tunnel, following the sweet smell of summer that had somehow followed him all the way down from the outside world. He ran and ran until he found himself back out in the sun and sat for a moment to catch his breath and take in the view from the hillside.

The sun was hanging in the afternoon sky with hardly a cloud for company. Down in the valley he could hear a lapwing calling as it swooped across the hillside just above the heather. Far away across the valley, he could see the smoking chimney of farmer Jones' farmhouse and the round top of the barn.

Farmer Jones' farm was very old and its crumbling stone buildings sagged. The bulging walls of the various farm buildings looked like fat bread cakes just taken from the oven to cool. The farm sat at the foot of a wooded hill with beech trees full of noisy crows. The field to the front of the farm was full of wheat yellowing in the sun with a dirt track running from the road and through the crop to the old house.

Albie started to run with a purpose. He ran and ran, jumping hedges and gates as he raced through fields and gardens at a gallop, until at last he found himself at the farm track. Kicking up dust as he made his way up to the house and past it to the barn.

Dirty and completely out of breath, Albie finally found himself standing on the cobblestone floor at the half open door. Cautiously he slipped into the barn, looking up at the neatly stacked fresh straw, he gave an urgent 'woof!' A second later it was answered with a chorus of enthusiastic yelping.

Albie clambered up the golden staircase of straw bales until he was looking down into a hollow in the straw dug out by Nellie. There lay Nellie in a nest of yellow straw suckling six newborn puppies!

Albie came to her and they greeted each other, licking one another's faces. One by one, Albie sniffed and licked all the new puppies. There were two just like him and two just like Nellie. As for the other two pups, one was all black with white paws that made her look like she had boots on and the last one, well he was just white all over.

Albie was very happy to finally find Nellie and his new family after searching all day. He couldn't wait to get them all back to their home by the fire in the kitchen. Albie thought about the adventures he'd had that day, the meadow, the beach, the angry butcher, the steam train, and Gwendolyn, the old dragon who lived inside the mountain. He then curled up next to Nellie and the puppies, closed his eyes and they all went to sleep.

Graffeg Children's Books

The White Hare

Nicola Davies

Illustrated by Anastasia Izlesou

Mother Cary's Butter Knife

Nicola Davies

Illustrated by Anja Uhren

Elias Martin

Nicola Davies

Illustrated by Fran Shum

The Selkie's Mate

Nicola Davies

Illustrated by Claire Jenkins

Bee Boy and the Moonflowers

Nicola Davies

Illustrated by Max Low

The Eel Question

Nicola Davies

Illustrated by Beth Holland

Perfect

Nicola Davies

Illustrated by Cathy Fisher

The Pond

Nicola Davies

Illustrated by Cathy Fisher

The Quiet Music of Gently Falling Snow

Jackie Morris

Illustrated by Jackie Morris

The Ice Bear

Jackie Morris

Illustrated by Jackie Morris

The Snow Leopard

Jackie Morris

Illustrated by Jackie Morris

Queen of the Sky

Jackie Morris

Illustrated by Jackie Morris

Through the Eyes of Me

Jon Roberts

Illustrated by Hannah Rounding

Animal Surprises

Nicola Davies

Illustrated by Abbie Cameron

The Word Bird

Nicola Davies

Illustrated by Abbie Cameron

Into the Blue

Nicola Davies

Illustrated by Abbie Cameron